nickelodeon

BIG TIME RUSH

P9-DDJ-581

SCHOLASTIC INC.
New York   Toronto   London   Auckland
Sydney   Mexico City   New Delhi   Hong Kong

ISBN 978-0-545-35846-0

Published by Scholastic Inc.
SCHOLASTIC and associated logos are trademarks and/or registered trademarks of Scholastic Inc.

12 11 10 9 8 7 6 5 4 3 2 1   11 12 13 14 15/0

Printed in the U.S.A.   40
First printing, September 2011

CONTENTS

INTRODUCTION

Gotta Live It Big Time

Can you feel the rush? The Big Time Rush, that is? Kendall Knight, Logan Mitchell, Carlos Garcia, and James Diamond are the four heartthrobs that make up this talented vocal group. Not only are they amazing singers—they're best friends, too.

These four guys were hockey-playing hunks in their small, snowy Minnesota hometown when a twist of fate changed their lives forever. James, following his dream of becoming a pop star, dragged his friends along with him to a nationwide talent search in their hometown. Record executive Gustavo Rocque was looking for the next big thing. But instead of choosing James, Gustavo was blown away by Kendall's incredible appeal and vocal talent. Gustavo immediately tried to lure Kendall out of Minnesota to the big lights of Los Angeles, but Kendall wasn't convinced. It took some encouragement from Logan, Carlos, and James (even though he was a little hurt at not being chosen) to get Kendall to consider it. This was a once-in-a-lifetime opportunity, after all.

Kendall had to make a choice. Should he move to the City of Angels to pursue a singing career or stay home in Minnesota with his best friends? Kendall decided to have the best of both worlds when he convinced Gustavo to help him form a singing super group with Logan, Carlos, and James! The foursome packed up and shipped out to LA to follow their dreams—and their lives have never been the same.

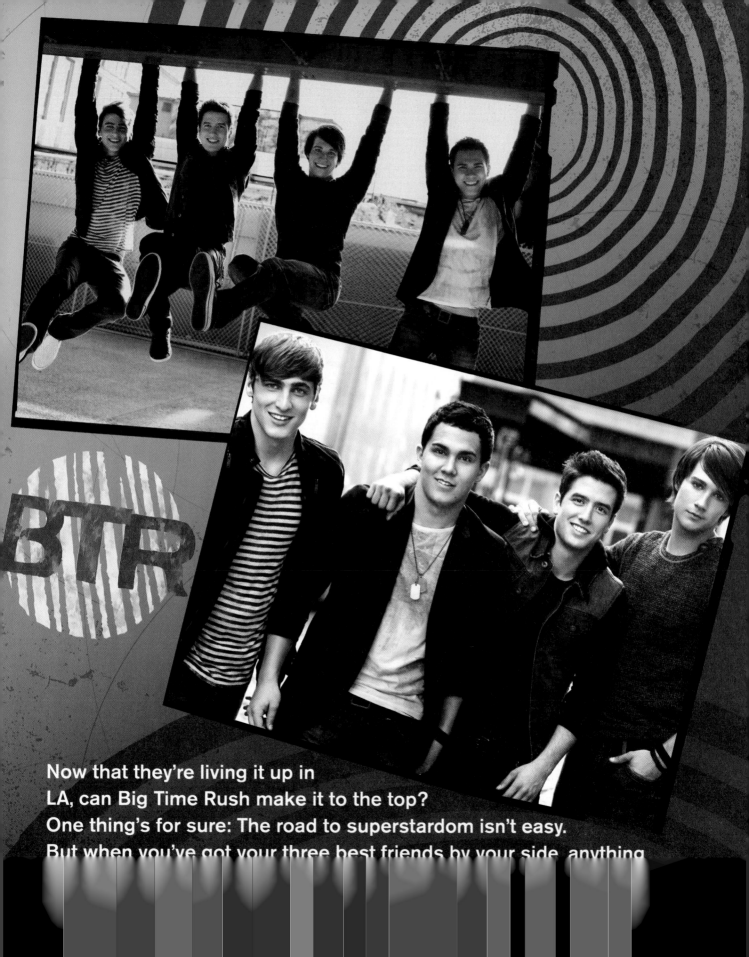

Now that they're living it up in
LA, can Big Time Rush make it to the top?
One thing's for sure: The road to superstardom isn't easy.
But when you've got your three best friends by your side, anything

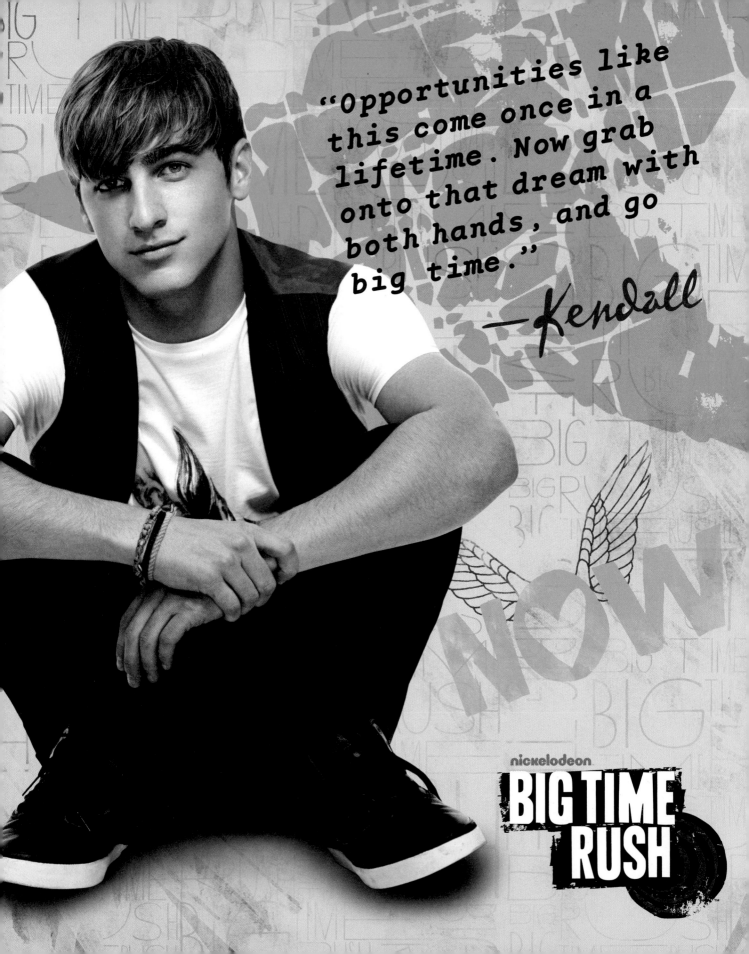

KENDALL

Kendall loves to hit the ice.

Kendall and Jo make a cute couple.

Kendall is tight with his mom and sister.

Kendall Knight is all cool charm and easy confidence. This big-hearted sweetie is happiest when he's just chilling with his boys or his best girl, Jo. He's a real family guy, too. His mom and his little sister, Katie, are very important to him.

Being part of a singing group wasn't always in Kendall's plans. He was happy being an all-star hockey player back in Minnesota before he was discovered. But like everything else in his life, Kendall knows how to roll with the punches. After all, a once-in-a-lifetime opportunity only comes . . . once in a lifetime! Now he's loving life in LA and working hard to help Big Time Rush top the charts.

With his all-star singing voice and his laid-back attitude, Kendall is a natural leader. His bandmates know they can count on him. And Kendall knows they've always got his back, too.

Are Logan and Camille "on" or "off" in this pic?

Total bookworm.

Logan has a seriously silly side.

LOGAN

Logan Mitchell is Big Time Rush's resident brainiac. But make no mistake about it—Logan is most definitely not a nerd. This adorable smart guy has got it all—intelligence, talent, and looks. When the band is in a jam, they know they can count on Logan's wits to get them out of trouble. He's a huge help when his friends need to get their homework done. And he's always willing to lend an ear and give great advice when it's needed.

While Logan can sometimes take life more seriously than the rest of the group, he still knows how to let loose and have a good time. He's down-to-earth, easy to talk to, and he's totally not afraid to show off his silly side. And in between reading books and acing his schoolwork, Logan even manages to make time for his on-and-off girlfriend, Camille.

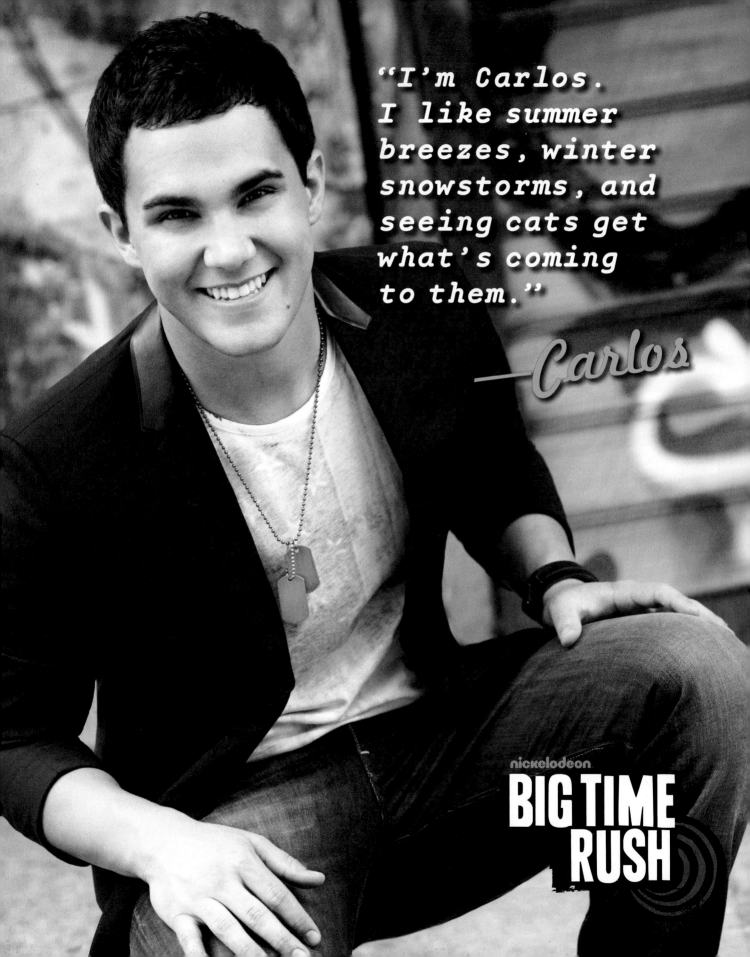

Carlos can't live without his helmet.

Carlos brings the party wherever he goes.

Fruit Smackers are Carlos' faves.

CARLOS

Carlos Garcia is a total goofball. He has an awesome sense of humor and loves to crack hilarious jokes and pull harmless pranks on his friends. This fun-loving guy can make anyone laugh. No matter how serious a situation, Carlos knows just how to lighten the mood with his funny ways and his contagious laugh. It seems like wherever Carlos goes, the good times follow.

Carlos wears his heart on his sleeve. Some might even call him a hopeless romantic, always looking for the right girl. He is really honest and he knows how to speak his mind—for better or worse. Although he has the best of intentions, sometimes his blabbermouth can get him into trouble. To make matters worse, he's quite the klutz. It's a good thing he wears his beloved hockey helmet so often!

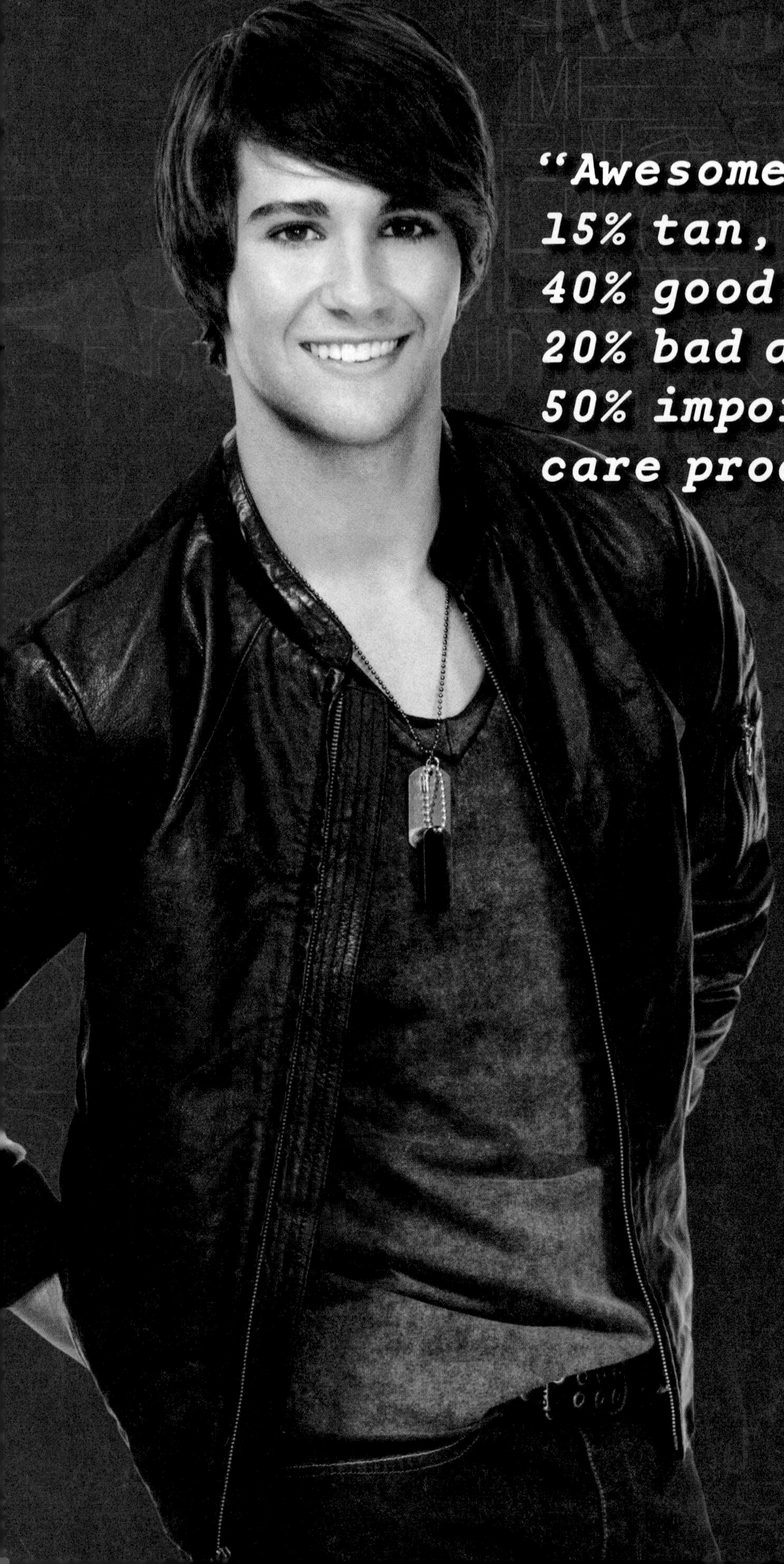

"Awesomeness is:
15% tan,
40% good attitude,
20% bad attitude, and
50% imported hair
care products."

—James

nickelodeon
BIG TIME RUSH

James likes what he sees.

JAMES

James Diamond is all about . . . James Diamond. James knows he's good-looking, and he's not afraid to flaunt it. He loves dressing in über-trendy clothes, and he exudes cool. He may not be a super genius like Logan, but that doesn't matter to him—just so long as he looks good (which he always does).

James may have a supersized ego, but his ridiculous overconfidence is always good for a laugh. Plus, James is a loyal friend and an extremely hard worker. He's willing to do whatever it takes to help Big Time Rush make it in Hollywood. After all, with his self-assuredness, this guy was built for stardom.

When James isn't staring lovingly at himself in the mirror, he's working his magic with the ladies. A real girls' guy, James is at his best when he's showing off his assets. Namely, his hair. James *loves* his hair.

Working on his tan.

This guy's already a star.

BIG TIME QUIZ: WHICH MEMBER OF BTR IS MOST LIKE YOU?

Kendall, Carlos, Logan, and James may be best buds, but when it comes down to it, they're four very different dudes. Their individuality gives Big Time Rush its strength! Ever wondered which one of the guys you have the most in common with? Take this quiz to find out!

1. Your favorite class at school is:

a. lunch. Okay, so it's not really a class—but you love socializing.

b. gym. It's the one class where you can be silly and it's okay!

c. math or science. These classes are tough for some, but they come naturally to you!

d. choir, drama, band—anywhere that you can receive praise for your (many) talents.

2. At school, you have a reputation for being:

a. an all-around nice person.

b. a class clown.

c. a smarty pants.

d. popular.

3. Your idea of the perfect vacation is:

a. going on a ski trip with a huge group of buddies.

b. riding death-defying roller coasters at a theme park.

c. traveling to far-off lands with lots of culture and history.

d. a trip to the beach to work on your tan.

4. You would describe your fashion sense as:

a. laid-back.

b. eccentric.

c. preppy.

d. super trendy.

5. To get ready for a night out, you:

a. hang out with a group of friends.

b. bring your A-game. If there's one thing you know how to do, it's have a good time!

c. listen to some music and relax.

d. dance in front of the mirror . . . alone.

6. You feel proudest when you:

a. do something good for someone else.

b. make someone laugh.

c. ace a test.

d. receive a compliment.

7. When you go to a party, you spend your time:

a. chatting with old friends.

b. telling jokes and funny stories.

c. having a deep, meaningful one-on-one conversation with someone.

d. talking at length about yourself.

8. When you're stressed out, you like to unwind by:

a. looking at old pictures with friends.

b. going to see a hilarious, laugh-out-loud movie.

c. reading a really good book.

d. pampering yourself with a day at the spa.

9. You believe true confidence:

a. is believing in yourself.

b. is being able to laugh at yourself.

c. comes from hard work.

d. comes from looking super hot.

10. If you get embarrassed, you:

a. brush it off. What's the point in letting it get you down?

b. laugh about it. Laugh, and the world laughs with you.

c. worry about it for a minute, then try to forget about it.

d. Embarrassed? I don't get embarrassed!

THE RESULTS!

If you answered mostly. . .

A's

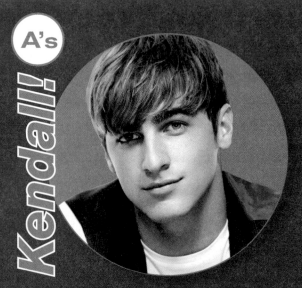

Kendall!

You're an all-around easygoing person. Friendship is incredibly important to you. You tend to bring people together.

B's

Carlos!

You're a total jokester, and nothing makes you happier than making people laugh. You love to have a good time.

C's

Logan!

You're super smart. You always manage to come up with a solution, even for the toughest problems. Your friends know they can count on you in a pinch.

D's

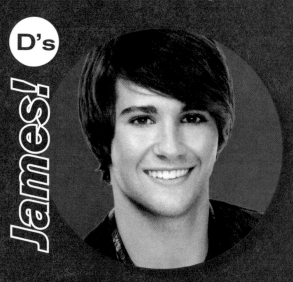

James!

You love to be in the spotlight, getting recognized for the super talented, charming, adorable person you know you are. Your confidence is contagious.

The Palm Woods

The California dream is a reality at the Palm Woods, where aspiring singers, actors, dancers, and other Hollywood hopefuls rest their talented heads. The Palm Woods is filled with luxurious living suites, a relaxing lounge and lobby area, and best of all, a shimmering, crystal-blue outdoor swimming pool.

The pool is the place to see and be seen at the Palm Woods. Whether you're going for a dip, working on your tan, or just hanging out with friends, this is where all the action's at. With giant umbrellas, comfy lounge chairs, and tables for group gatherings, the pool is always sun-filled *and* fun-filled.

Big Time Rush's apartment at the Palm Woods is out of this world. They share the apartment with Kendall's mom and Katie, but there's more than enough space for everyone. With arcade video games, a hockey table, and several computers, the guys have everything they could possibly need. They even have a slide in the middle of their apartment!

The guys of Big Time Rush have a pretty busy schedule. On weekdays they attend the Palm Woods School. For four hours each day, Miss Collins teaches them math, science, English, and other school subjects. Then they head to work at Rocque Records for the rest of their day. With such a tough schedule, it's a good thing they can head back to the pool to unwind!

The Palm Woods Family

KATIE

Big Time Rush would be completely lost without Kendall's little sis, Katie. Katie is full of spunk and energy, and she's always there to get the guys out of trouble—which is often. Of course she'd rather be playing with her friends, beating a video game, or coming up with her latest money-making scheme, but helping out the guys comes first. Katie is smart, and she doesn't take flak from anyone. Especially Mr. Bitters, the Palm Woods manager. Quick on her feet, Katie is always ready with a snappy comeback. This girl may be little in stature, but she sure can fend for herself!

Katie's latest money-making scheme.

Katie knows how to get what she wants.

Katie doesn't take flak from anyone!

"I am loving this town, so the guys better not blow it."

—Katie

MRS. KNIGHT

"If a girl doesn't accept you for who you are, then maybe she's not the right girl for you."

—Mrs. Knight

Kendall's mom is a total sweetheart. She came out to Los Angeles to chaperone her son and his three best friends while they pursue fame and fortune. She's like a second mom to Logan, Carlos, and James while they are away from their own families. Mrs. Knight is the mom any kid wants—kind, patient, and supportive of her kids' dreams. She gives great advice. But she can occasionally be a little bit overprotective, and sometimes she worries about the kids too much. From time to time, she questions the guys' weird antics—as any mother would. Ultimately, she just wants the very best for them!

MR. BITTERS

"Have a Palm Woods day!"

—Mr. Bitters

MANAGER

The only downside to living at the Palm Woods is the building manager, Mr. Bitters. Mr. Bitters is, well . . . bitter! This cranky dude is always trying to put a damper on Big Time Rush's fun. Sure, the guys may bend the rules from time to time, accidentally break stuff at the Palm Woods, and almost never listen to Bitters. But the guys just can't help messing with him. It's too easy!

The Palm Woods Girls

CAMILLE

Camille is an actress at the Palm Woods, and she truly dedicates herself to her craft. When Camille gets a new role, she dives completely into that character. That means walking around the Palm Woods in full-on costume and reciting her lines to anyone she sees. As a result, she can be a little unpredictable—and often very kooky. For some reason, she tends to take parts that involve drama. A lot of drama! And, much to Big Time Rush's dismay, she often brings the drama around them!

Once you get past Camille's acting antics, she's a loyal, funny friend. She'll help out Big Time Rush any way she can, especially if it involves her acting skills. Camille has had a crush on Logan from day one, and the two have been an on-and-off couple for some time. But whether they're on or off, this drama queen always makes things interesting!

Camille is always ready to audition!

"It's a big audition. I play a princess-bot who falls for a super-handsome hair-model-spy-prince."

—Camille

JO

"Do you like ballet dancing, fine arts, or Scandinavian cheese?"

— Jo

BTR

Jo is the person that every girl wants to be and every guy wants to date. She's a talented actress, and she is completely down-to-earth and super sweet. When Jo first moved to the Palm Woods from her home in North Carolina, all the guys from Big Time Rush were head-over-heels. They all wanted to date her, but she told them she had a boyfriend back home. As it turned out, she didn't really have a boyfriend at all—she just wanted to put her acting career first. But, eventually, Kendall stole her heart, and now they're a devoted couple. And Jo's career has really taken off! She stars on the hit television show, *New Town High*, she has tons of loyal fans, and her face can often be found on the covers of magazines.

Jo makes a big first impression.

Jo loves to dance to Big Time Rush's music.

Dressing in disguise to avoid the paparazzi!

The Rest of the Palm Woods Gang

The Palm Woods is full of aspiring stars and kooky characters! Here's a look at some of the guys' favorite residents.

GUITAR DUDE

This guy is so laid-back, he doesn't even go by a real name! Guitar Dude is a songwriter, and he can often be found strumming his guitar by the pool.

"What's up, what's up, what's up?"

—Guitar Dude

THE JENNIFERS

The Jennifers are a clique of three singing, dancing, and acting girls—all named Jennifer, of course. This tight-knit group thinks pretty highly of themselves, and they rarely give Big Time Rush the time of day.

"If it seems harsh, it is, and so is this town."

—one of the Jennifers

TYLER

Tyler attends classes with Katie and the boys. He's in Hollywood to be an actor, but it's really his mom's dream, not his. Luckily, with the help of Big Time Rush, he's able to avoid going to most of his auditions!

"I don't want to be an actor. I want to be a kid."

—Tyler

LIGHTNING THE TV WONDER DOG

"Bark! Bark!"

—Lightning

Lightning isn't just a pet. He's a television action hero!

BUDDHA BOB

Buddha Bob is the Palm Woods groundskeeper and janitor. He's one strange guy. He has a deep voice, and he loves to give out karmic advice to the residents.

"Hey, fellas. I hear you've got a nasty clog."

—Buddha Bob

Rocque Records

Rocque Records is Big Time Rush's record label. It's headed up by Gustavo Rocque, Big Time Rush's boss. His assistant, Kelly Wainwright, is always around to lend a hand, too. Rocque Records is where Big Time Rush records all its songs and albums.

GUSTAVO

Gustavo Rocque is the brains behind Rocque Records. He's known in the music business as a songwriting genius and a multimillionaire mega producer who has launched many boy bands onto the music charts. Some of his famous boy band creations include Boyquake, Boys in the Attic, and Boyzcity.

Gustavo can be tough, and he demands hard work and results from the members of Big Time Rush. To say Gustavo has some anger management issues is an understatement. One time his temper got so out of control that it caused a small earthquake to shake LA! But deep down, he's got a big heart, and he always manages to get the best out of the band.

"I could turn a dog into a pop star."

—Gustavo

KELLY

"Okay, guys . . . It's time to hit the studio."

—Kelly

Kelly Wainwright is Gustavo's loyal assistant. Kelly's usually the voice of reason at Rocque Records. Whenever Gustavo's temper flares up or Big Time Rush is goofing off, Kelly's the one with her head on straight. She has loads of patience, which comes in handy when you work for someone like Gustavo. And she often finds herself settling problems between Gustavo and Big Time Rush. Sure, Kelly gets frustrated now and then. But she loves her job, so it's totally worth it.

GRIFFIN

Arthur Griffin is the fourth most powerful CEO in America, and he's the head of Rocque Records, as well as many other companies in the entertainment industry. He's all about making money, money, and more money. He sees Big Time Rush as little more than a dollar-making machine. And he'll fire anyone on the spot if they don't deliver. Needless to say, Griffin's not so good with the warm-fuzzies. But, hey, he's the boss.

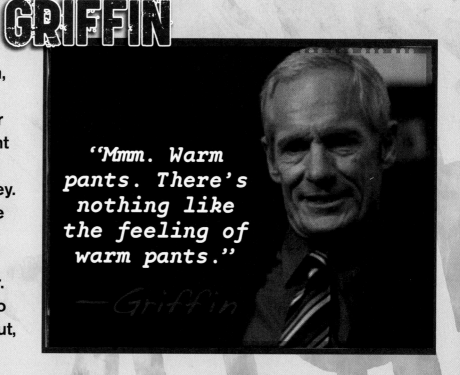

"Mmm. Warm pants. There's nothing like the feeling of warm pants."

—Griffin

Big Time Hits

Big Time Rush has recorded many hit singles with Gustavo and Rocque Records. Some of their best hits include:

"Big Time Rush"

Song Meaning: Big Time Rush's first single is all about following your dreams and doing whatever it takes to make them come true. Follow your heart, give it your all, and go for it! What have you got to lose?

"Boyfriend"

Song Meaning: This song is about a guy who has a crush on a girl. He hears she's looking for a boyfriend, and he wants to be the one. This song is asking her to put her trust in him and give him a chance.

"'Til I Forget About You"

Song Meaning: This song tells the story of someone who has had his heart broken. And the best way to get over a breakup is to go out and have a good time dancing, laughing, and partying with friends.

"City Is Ours"

Song Meaning: When you're Big Time Rush, there's nothing like putting on a rockin', sold-out show after a tough day. That's what this song is all about—how love from your adoring fans can turn anything around.

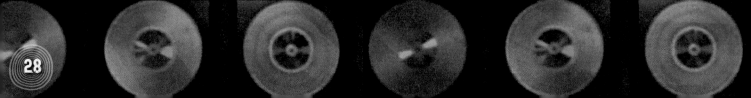

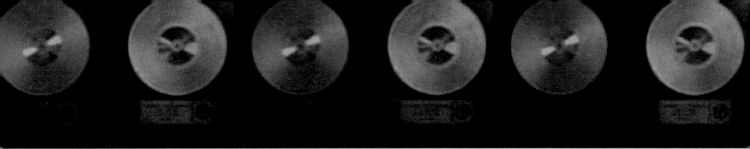

"Nothing Even Matters"

Song Meaning: According to this song, your problems don't mean a thing so long as you've got the person you love by your side. When it comes down to it, that's the only thing that matters.

"Halfway There"

Song Meaning: Friendship is number one to Big Time Rush. This song is about how much easier it is to get where you want to go when your friends help you along the way.

"Big Night"

Song Meaning: When you've been working hard all day and you're feeling down, it's time for a pick-me-up. And what better way to get happy than to get dressed up, grab your friends, and dance the night away?

"Count on You"

Song Meaning: Big Time Rush recorded this track with songstress Jordin Sparks. It's about having been in love and getting your heart broken, and learning to trust again.

"Any Kind of Guy"

Song Meaning: This song is about a guy who is willing to change everything about himself to be with the girl he likes. He'll go anywhere, near or far, just to have the chance to make her happy.

"Famous"

Song Meaning: If fame's your game, then go for it! But you've got to put in the work to make it big. Big Time Rush knows that nothing's handed to you on a silver platter, and they sing all about it in this song.

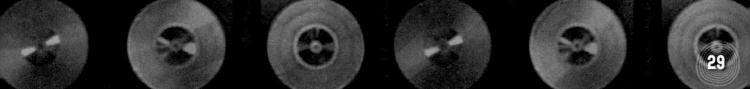

Big Time True or False

Can you tell what's fact and what's fiction when it comes to Big Time Rush? Put your Big Time Rush knowledge to the test by deciding whether each of the following statements is true or false!

1. When Gustavo made the kids go to school at the School of Rocque, he hired an action movie star to be their teacher.

TRUE or FALSE?

2. When Jo first moved to the Palm Woods, Logan pretended to be a spy to impress her.

TRUE or FALSE?

3. Gustavo has a hairless cat.

TRUE or FALSE?

4. James was once orange because he used self-tanning spray.

TRUE or FALSE?

5. At the Palm Woods School, Miss Collins lets the kids have class in the pool.

TRUE or FALSE?

6. Griffin likes to wear warm pants.

TRUE or FALSE?

7. James once booked a job as a hand model.

TRUE or FALSE?

8. Mrs. Knight once thought Buddha Bob was an axe murderer.

TRUE or FALSE?

9. When the Jennifers lost one of their clan, they made Carlos into a Jennifer.

TRUE or FALSE?

10. Katie secretly has a huge crush on James.

TRUE or FALSE?

Big Time Quotes

Who said that? Match the quotation with the person who spoke it.

Katie

Gustavo

Griffin

James

Jo

Kendall

Carlos

Mr. Bitters

Camille

Logan

1. *"We'll all wear bandannas. It could be our 'thing.' Bandannas!"*

2. *"A week ago we were a hockey team in Minnesota and today we're a band in LA. Anything is possible."*

3. *"I'm going to see 'The Solar Winds of Venus' exhibit at the planetarium. You wanna come with?"*

4. *"How dare you? What we had was real, but you threw it all away for Trish! I never want to see you again, Troy! NEVER!"*

5. *"This looks like a job for El Hombre de Flaming Space Rock Man!"*

6. *"You have a gift. You have the fire. You also have anger management issues. Some people say I have anger management issues, but I also have FIVE HOUSES!"*

7. *"Hey, I'm a preteen girl and he's a cute pop star. I'm not made of stone, you know."*

8. *"I hate hockey."*

9. *"Watching you boys go from nobodies to somebodies has been more thrilling than hunting humans."*

10. *"They destroyed the Palm Woods computerized registration system, two lamps, three vases, and my pants!"*

Big Time Trivia

How well do you really know Big Time Rush? Try your hand at these multiple choice questions:

1. When Big Time Rush thinks there's a ghost at the Palm Woods, it turns out to be:

a. *Mr. Bitters trying to scare everyone.*

b. *the new girl practicing for an acting role.*

c. *Gustavo sleepwalking.*

d. *Buddha Bob patrolling the grounds.*

2. When Katie auditions for a Suds-O laundry detergent commercial, she doesn't get the part because:

a. *she makes fun of the product during her audition.*

b. *she gets in a fight with another kid in the waiting room.*

c. *she decides to launch her own line of laundry detergent.*

d. *she shows up to the audition with a giant stain on her shirt.*

3. When Jo moves to the Palm Woods, the Big Time Rush guys like her because:

a. *she's from North Carolina.*

b. *she's nice.*

c. *she's not crazy.*

d. *all of the above.*

4. Which of the following roles has Camille *not* auditioned for:

a. *a robot princess.*

b. *a wrestler.*

c. *a witch.*

d. *a construction worker.*

5. When Big Time Rush mansion-sits for Gustavo, which animal gets stuck in his bathroom?

a. *a sewer rat.*

b. *a hairless cat.*

c. *an alligator.*

d. *a rhinoceros.*

6. When Griffin takes over Big Time Rush's photo shoot for *Pop Tiger* magazine, he makes them dress like:

a. *space matadors.*

b. *superheroes.*

c. *cowboy robots.*

d. *werewolves.*

7. When Big Time Rush organizes the school dance, where do they hold it?

a. their apartment.

b. the Palm Woods pool.

c. Rocque Records.

d. a bowling alley.

8. What is the name of Big Time Rush's choreographer?

a. Mr. X.

b. Super G.

c. Big Daddy.

d. Rockin' Brock.

9. Big Time Rush's favorite meal is Mrs. Knight's famous:

a. fish sticks and tater tots.

b. homemade lasagna.

c. roast leg of lamb.

d. meatloaf.

10. Which of the following has *not* been one of Katie's money-making schemes:

a. selling snow cones at the Palm Woods pool.

b. starting a Palm Woods beauty service.

c. betting on card games with the Palm Woods housekeeping staff.

d. making a VIP room at the Palm Woods pool and charging kids for entry.

Big Time Love

Now for some fun fill-ins! These questions don't have right or wrong answers. Just answer them honestly!

Who is your favorite member of Big Time Rush–Logan, Carlos, James, or Kendall?_____

Which Palm Woods girl do you think you'd be friends with–Katie, Camille, Jo, or the Jennifers?

_____

What's your favorite Big Time Rush song? _____

If you could be famous, what would you be famous for? _____

If you had your own band, which friends would you ask to join you? _____

What would you name your band? _____

If your band could cover a song by any artist for your album, what would you sing? _____

_____

Big Time True or False
ANSWERS:

1. False! Gustavo hired a wrestler to be the guys' teacher.

2. False! Logan pretended to have a British accent to impress Jo.

3. True.

4. True.

5. False! Palm Woods School at the pool was just Big Time Rush's fantasy.

6. True.

7. False! James once booked a gig as an elbow model!

8. True.

9. True.

10. False! As if! Katie's heart belongs to pop star Dak Zevon.

Big Time Quotes
ANSWERS:

1. James

2. Kendall

3. Logan

4. Camille

5. Carlos

6. Gustavo

7. Katie

8. Jo

9. Griffin

10. Mr. Bitters

Big Time Trivia
ANSWERS:

1. b

2. b

3. d

4. d

5. c

6. a

7. c

8. a

9. a

10. b

Big Time Party

For the launch of Big Time Rush's first album, Gustavo threw a party! But Big Time Rush didn't make it on the guest list. "It's a classy party for executives only," Gustavo explained to the guys. They were pretty bummed and did their best to get themselves invited. "Fine, you can stay, but do not go in my Super Party Fun Box," said Gustavo. Of course, the guys couldn't resist seeing what was inside. But once they went in the box, they soon realized it had been a trick! When they got out Gustavo had sent them back to their apartment!

If the guys couldn't go to their own party, they'd just have to throw one themselves! But since it's a Palm Woods rule not to have parties (and if the guys got another strike they would be kicked out of Palm Woods), they decided to have a small "get-together" instead. Piece of cake!

The get-together was underway, and everyone was having a great time—except Logan. He had two girls after him! But Logan decided to make the best of it, flirting with both Camille and Mercedes . . . until they found out—and tossed Logan into the pool!

Camille was pretty upset. "I'm not talking to you for one whole week," she said. "But we could still dance." Things were looking up for Logan after all!

The get-together soon turned into a full-blown party when Carlos accidentally invited all his phone contacts! To make matters worse, Mr. Bitters suspected a party was going on. Luckily, Jo and Kendall distracted Bitters, by luring him into Gustavo's Super Party Fun Box. Party on!

Meanwhile, Gustavo's party was a bust. Griffin was bored almost to tears. "I'd rather watch a Dutchman make molasses," he said. Finally, Gustavo admitted that he had thrown the worst party ever. So he brought his party to Big Time Rush's bash at the Palm Woods! Problem solved.

Big Time Rush's party was a hit. As Carlos and James put it, "We're the Hollywood super party kings of Hollywood!"

LIVE IT
BIG TIME

Big Time Jobs

One time, Kendall, Logan, Carlos, and James had a foot race at the Palm Woods— and they crashed into Mr. Bitters' reception desk, causing $2,000 worth of damage!

Gustavo paid Bitters back, but he made the guys get jobs to cover the cost. And that wasn't all. "Until you pay me back, you will not dip a toe into your beloved Palm Woods pool!" he threatened. The guys got to work right away!

Carlos got a job as a production assistant for Gustavo. When Gustavo asked Carlos to get him a cup of coffee, it should have been an easy job. "One coffee, coming right up!" said Carlos. But the coffee machine was possessed! It wouldn't stop making foam! When the foam threatened to take over the building, Kelly helped Carlos smash the expensive coffee maker to bits.

James decided to use his good looks to make some money. James signed Katie up as his agent. "We'll need new headshots, new clothes, some personal stylists," Katie advised.

After all that, she got James a job as an elbow model for skin cream. But it turned out Katie had spent more on James' headshots, clothes, and stylists than what the modeling gig paid!

Meanwhile, Logan and Kendall decided to try babysitting, but it paid terribly. "At this rate, we're still not gonna pay Gustavo back anytime soon," said Logan. So Kendall and Logan decided to watch a bunch of kids at once—but they were out of control! Kendall's mom said they needed to keep the kids occupied. That's when they got a brilliant idea: Why not have the kids hold a car wash?

The car wash wound up making tons of money. Plus, the kids were so tired afterward that they even took naps! It all worked out great, except . . . whoops—Kendall and Logan used soap and materials from the Palm Woods to wash the cars, and Mr. Bitters wanted them to pay him back.

All in all, the guys ended up spending more money than they made at their various jobs. Gustavo completely lost his cool, smashing up the Rocque Records studio. Plus Griffin wanted Gustavo to pay him back for all the damage! In the end, everyone came together to host a giant car wash to make back the money they had lost.

Big Time Video

"Every time you hear crying and the squeak of luggage, another Hollywood dream has been crushed," Buddha Bob told Big Time Rush. It's too bad the squeaking luggage belonged to the band's friend, Camille. "I haven't booked a part in six months and my dad's making me move back to Connecticut!" Camille sobbed.

At the same time, Big Time Rush was filming their first music video for their song, "City Is Ours." They told Camille she could have a part! There was just one problem: Gustavo didn't want Camille in the video. "This is a music video. Not a charity case!" he said.

A bunch of directors came to Rocque Records to pitch ideas for the music video. A fashion photographer named Marcos del Posey really wanted to direct the video—but Gustavo didn't like his concept. Marcos was devastated.

Things kept getting worse for the band as they promised more and more Palm Woods friends that they could be in the video. They felt awful about lying, but at the same time they wanted to help their friends.

BIG TIME RUSH

Finally, the guys decided to direct their own fake music video. "It's not lying if we put all of them in a video," said Kendall. "That's all the parents need to see: their kids 'acting' in Hollywood." The guys filmed a video and showed it to their friends in the Palm Woods lobby. It didn't turn out as they'd hoped since they lacked the proper video cameras and didn't really plan out the shots. "That is the worst music video ever," said the Jennifers.

Wannabe-director Marcos just so happened to be in the lobby when the guys were showing their music video. Marcos agreed that the video was awful, but he liked their concept. "Flash party was inspired. What you need is a pretty, pretty roof."

The boys decided to hire Marcos to direct their video. They just needed a pretty, pretty car. Luckily, Katie knew just where they could get one: Mr. Bitters.

Marcos filmed the video, and Gustavo loved it. He even decided to buy Mr. Bitters' car to be the official Big Time Rush vehicle! In the end, the guys scored a sweet ride and got to help out a good friend. "Looks like we're staying at the Palm Woods for a while," Camille's dad told her.

Big Time Fans

The Big Time Rush guys love fan mail. But Gustavo once shared some words of wisdom about responding to letters. "Don't give out advice, otherwise some crazed fan will show up on your doorstep and ask you to help make them famous."

At that moment, Jenny Tinkler, an old friend from Minnesota, arrived. "I picked up everything and moved to LA so you can help me be famous like you promised!" It seemed Carlos responded to Jenny's fan letter and offered to help make her dreams come true. Whoops!

The guys adored Jenny, and she had a gorgeous singing voice, but disaster followed her wherever she went. "Remember the second grade, when she broke my arm playing marbles?" asked James. "Or the fifth grade, when she gave me the first paper cut in history that required surgery?" Ouch.

So it's no surprise that Jenny had a crazy trombone accident that made the Rocque Records air conditioner go haywire. And Death Smash—"the world's most destructive band"— was not happy about it! "If you don't fix the fan right quick," threatened the lead singer, "I'm gonna show you how destructive we can get."

Meanwhile, Mr. Bitters kicked Jenny out of the Palm Woods. "Your friend has been here for two hours and so far has trashed an elevator, broken a water main, ruined my favorite pen, and started two fires!" he exclaimed. The guys felt terrible. They didn't want to break their promise to Jenny!

Over at Rocque Records, the air conditioner was still broken. The lead singer of Death Smash decided to fix it himself, but he got sucked into the air vent! Then his bandmates refused to go on tour without him. "I guess we'll have to cancel the European tour unless an amazing lead singer who's super destructive just falls from the sky."

Just then, Jenny literally fell through the ceiling. Death Smash decided to take her on tour. And Big Time Rush fulfilled their promise of helping a friend make it in LA!

RIGHT HERE AND NOW!!!

Big Time Live

For a performance on A.M.L.A., Los Angeles' number one morning show, the guys had to get up at five in the morning. The show's producer, Jane Kennedy, introduced herself to the band and showed them to their awesome green room. It was filled with all kinds of breakfast food and goodies! But the appeal of tasty treats soon faded as the show started to run long. All of a sudden, Jane went from nice to nasty. "You guys are cut," she said.

The guys were devastated, but Jane didn't care. "LA needs their traffic, weather, stock reports, celebrity interviews, and cooking tips. What they don't need is to see a stupid boy band." Sheesh, that was harsh! But Big Time Rush didn't get up at five a.m. to be treated like this! They were determined to find a way to cut four minutes from Jane's show—whether she liked it or not!

Back at Rocque Records, Griffin gave Gustavo and Kelly employee evaluations. They were failing miserably, and Griffin threatened to give the Rocque Records offices to another company.

"If you don't give me a grade A performance, I'm going to give this centrally located and expensive office to someone who can!" he said. Oh, no. Now Gustavo and Kelly were banking on Big Time Rush to put on an amazing performance on the morning show—or their offices were on the line!

Over at A.M.L.A., the boys hijacked the teleprompter. They added their performance back into the show's lineup, and they sped up the teleprompter to make the show's host read faster! Soon, producer Jane figured out what was going on and sent security after the guys.

The guys convinced Katie to distract all the security guards in the building by leading them on a low-speed golf cart chase! Meanwhile, Big Time Rush took over the show. Carlos did the cooking segment. Logan gave the financial report. And James delivered the weather.

All the while, Jane was losing her mind! Until she was taken out by Katie on her golf cart. Oops! The guys got their chance and launched into their latest single, "'Til I Forget About You." The song was a hit and song downloads went through the roof! Griffin was pleased, and Gustavo and Kelly passed their evaluation and got to keep their offices.

BIG TIME RUSH